My Princess Collection

Alice

A Most Wonderful Adventure

Book Six

Written by M. L. Dunham

For information address Disney Press, 114 Fifth Avenue,
New York, New York 10011-5690.
Printed in China
First Edition
13 15 17 19 20 18 16 14 12
ISBN 978-1-4231-2565-5

T425-2382-5 12196

For more Disney Press fun,
visit www.disneybooks.com

Chapter One

Oh, hello, there. My name is Alice, and I'd love to tell you about a most wonderful adventure I once had. It all started when I was rather bored . . . and curious.

You see, one day, my older sister was giving me a history lesson outdoors. Now, I don't know about you, but I find history lessons rather boring to begin with, and when you're outside, listening to one . . . well, there do tend to be a lot of distractions.

In my case, I just happened to see a white rabbit run by. And he was no ordinary white rabbit, mind you! He was dressed quite formally, he carried a gold pocket watch, and he kept saying over and over, "I'm late! I'm late!"

Now, I'd like to ask you a simple question: who wouldn't want to follow such a curious fellow to find out what was going on? So I did.

Chapter Two

The next thing I knew, I was tumbling down a very deep hole. I wasn't hurt, but I was rather concerned about how I might get out. I knew that I must find the White Rabbit, so that he could show me the way home. As I followed him, however, he kept going through doors, which got smaller and smaller, until I was simply too big to follow him.

It was then that the Doorknob on that last door gave me some advice: "Why don't you try the bottle on the table?"

Sure enough, there was a bottle with a label that read DRINK ME. So I did.

And, oh, my! Immediately, I shrank to a tiny size, which allowed me to go through the door into Wonderland.

Chapter Three

Once there, I found myself drifting on a vast sea. I ran into a dodo bird that was floating on the sea—on top of a toucan! He was of no use at all in helping me find my way. But I must say he was rather amusing, and it made things a tiny bit exciting to see such an oddity. Of course, that was only the beginning. . . .

Soon I came ashore where I met twins named Tweedledum and Tweedledee. They began to tell me a story—which started out quite pleasantly, but turned out to be quite tragic and sad (it was about some baby oysters' being eaten by a hungry and conniving walrus). It was simply awful!

Of course, I decided it best to move on, and at last I found the White Rabbit. He was thoroughly confused and kept calling me Mary Ann. At any rate, once I followed him inside his house, I ran into a terrible dilemma—I ate the wrong thing and become enormous again. Luckily, I grabbed ahold of a carrot from the White Rabbit's garden, took a bite . . . and became tiny again. Would I ever be the right size in this strange land?

Chapter Four

Next, I met some nasty giant flowers. (Actually, I'm quite sure they were of normal size; it was I who was tiny.)

One of them, Iris, whispered to the others, "She's nothing but a common weed!"

Of all the cruel things to say! Needless to say, I moved on very quickly, indeed.

After more meetings with more nonsensical creatures, I found myself in the woods and began to feel quite lost. All of a sudden, I could have sworn I heard a voice talking to me. So I looked behind a nearby tree trunk. But no one was there.

"Lose something?" the voice asked. I looked up and saw a strange, moon-shaped object in the tree.

It was the Cheshire Cat. He had been the one talking all along, I suppose, just to tease me. He had pink and purple stripes and an absolutely mocking grin. But he did have some advice (even though it came out in the form of ridiculous riddles).

The Cheshire Cat directed me toward the Mad Hatter's tea party. There, things became more and more curious—especially after the Mad Hatter insisted on celebrating all our unbirthdays. I, myself, began to feel rather silly.

That's when things truly began to get crazy. The party went from being celebrated around the table to being celebrated atop, and then even above, the table. I really had no idea what to make of it all.

I was beginning to lose hope of ever finding
my way, when suddenly the White Rabbit
appeared again! Of course, he ran off, but at
least I had a chance to follow him—for a bit.
He was quite fast, you know, and soon I found
myself at a crossroads, with no idea as to
which way to go.

Chapter Five

At last, the Cheshire Cat appeared again and let me through a door in his tree. I ended up in the Queen of Hearts's garden, playing croquet.

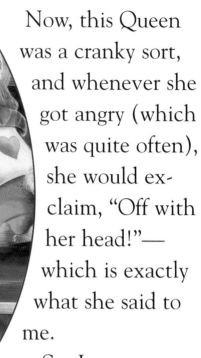

Now, this Queen was a cranky sort, and whenever she got angry (which was quite often), she would exclaim, "Off with her head!"— which is exactly what she said to me.

So, I went on trial and was truly in danger of having my head lopped off, when the Cheshire Cat appeared once again, along with several of the friends whom I had met during my travels. They caused such confusion that soon I was able to escape and run far away.

Chapter Six

I ran as fast as I could all the way through Wonderland until I reached the very same tiny door through which I had entered at the beginning of my adventure. And quite to my surprise, when I opened the door, I saw myself fast asleep! Not knowing what else to do, I shouted. And do you know, I actually managed to wake myself up! At last, the horrible dream was over!

It was so good to be back home finally. And although my adventure wasn't entirely pleasant, I am delighted to say that once upon a time, I had the most incredible adventure in a magical place called Wonderland. And who knows? Maybe someday I'll visit again!